MARY-KATE AND ASHLEY

IN ACTION

D0005559

The Dream Team

A Novelization by Megan Stine
based on the teleplay
by Dianne Dixon

📚 HarperEntertainment
An Imprint of HarperCollins*Publishers*

A PARACHUTE PRESS BOOK

A PARACHUTE PRESS BOOK

Parachute Publishing, L.L.C.
156 Fifth Avenue, Suite 302
New York, NY 10010

Published by
⚒HarperEntertainment
An Imprint of HarperCollins*Publishers*
10 East 53rd Street, New York, NY 10022-5299

CHAPTER ONE
A Surprise Call

"Wow! Check this out," Mary-Kate said. She flopped down on a leather sofa beside her sister, Ashley.

The two girls were flying home in their private jet. They had just finished their latest assignment—as special agents! Now that their work was done, they could finally kick back and relax.

Ashley glanced up from the book she was writing in. "What is it?" she asked.

"It's a minidisk with all kinds of different music beats!" Mary-Kate explained. "It has salsa and Latin rhythms— even Polish polkas! Want to hear?"

"Polkas?" Ashley made a face. "Sorry. Not for me."

"Suit yourself," Mary-Kate said. "I'll

just listen to it on my headphones." She grabbed her ultra-small minidisk player from the coffee table.

Ashley put her pen down and read over her notes. "Did you know we've flown to over twenty countries on secret missions so far?" she asked.

"Really?" Mary-Kate asked. "Time flies when you're having fun!"

Ashley loved collecting interesting facts. Mary-Kate thought it was a weird habit, but sometimes it came in handy during assignments.

Ashley sighed and stretched her arms. "This is great. I love it when the jet's on autopilot. We get to chill, and with any luck we'll be home in time for that great slumber party this weekend!"

Quincy, the girls' beige Scottie, jumped onto the sofa next to Mary-Kate. Quincy looked like an ordinary dog, but he was really a high-tech special agent assisting machine!

"I need some chill-out time myself," he said.

"Quincy," Ashley scolded gently. "You know you don't belong on the couch."

"No fair," Quincy grumbled. "I'm a robot. Not a dog. I don't even shed! Why can't I sit on the furniture?"

"Because your claws are scratching the leather," Mary-Kate answered.

Wham! The cabin door burst open. Rodney Choy ran into the jet's living room. "Ashley! Mary-Kate! Headquarters called. They need two special agents right away. And they need the best!"

Rod worked with Mary-Kate and Ashley. He flew with them on all their secret missions, and drove them wherever they needed to go.

Mary-Kate flipped open her high-tech special-agent bracelet. She pressed the record button. "Digital diary entry—Friday, five P.M. Good-bye, slumber party. Hello, new assignment!"

"Where are we going this time?" Ashley asked.

Rod flicked on the TV. "There." He pointed to the picture on the screen. "To the Global Games—in Rome!"

"Awesome!" Ashley shouted. "Did you know that Rome is one of the oldest cities in the world? It's been around since 753 B.C.!"

Mary-Kate turned to Rod. "So what's the assignment?"

"There's a problem with the gymnastics

team from a country called Hipslovia," Rod reported. "No one can beat them. They look super-human."

Mary-Kate and Ashley studied the Hipslovian gymnasts on the screen. All seven of them were tall and thin. They wore matching red and yellow workout suits. And every one of them flipped, spun, and jumped with super-human strength!

"Rod is right—they are unbelievable!" Ashley said.

"So what's our next move?" Mary-Kate asked.

Ivan Quintero hurried into the living room. Mary-Kate and Ashley called him IQ for short.

IQ was the same age as Mary-Kate and Ashley. He invented all of Mary-Kate and Ashley's special-agent gear. He had even invented Quincy!

IQ ran his fingers through his spiky brown hair. "Here's the scoop. You two are going undercover as members of the U.S. gymnastics team."

"Great!" Mary-Kate cheered.

"See that girl?" IQ pointed at the TV. A stocky gymnast appeared on the screen. Her face was grumpy. And her feet were huge.

"She doesn't look like the other gymnasts," Ashley said.

IQ nodded. "That's Grudmilla, the Hipslovian team's captain. You'll have to keep a close eye on her."

A gymnast in a red, white, and blue leotard appeared on the screen. Her long blond hair was pulled back into a ponytail.

"Hey, look! That's Lauren Andersen," Mary-Kate said. "She's totally awsome!"

"You're right," IQ continued. "If the Hipslovians want to win, they have to beat Lauren. She's the United States' best chance to win a gold medal."

"Your job is to protect Lauren—and to find out how the Hipslovian team is doing those amazing moves," Rod said. "Because if they're cheating, none of the other teams has a fair chance!"

"We're ready," Ashley said.

Mary-Kate turned to IQ with a big smile. "Show us the toys."

Ashley laughed. "With Mary-Kate, it's all about the special-agent gear."

IQ pulled out a pair of glittery hairclips. "These are clip-cams," he explained, "hairclips with tiny video cameras hidden inside. Flip them on, and you can tape whatever you see."

"That's so cool!" Mary-Kate said. She grabbed one of the clips and stuck it in her hair.

"Perfect!" Ashley agreed. "And, of course, we have our special-agent bracelets."

IQ nodded. "As always, your bracelets are a calendar, address book, minicomputer,

digital diary, radar detector, and cell phone all rolled into one. Plus, if you attach the clip-cams to your bracelets, you can play videos or local radio stations."

"Cool," Mary-Kate agreed.

"Looks like we're all set," Ashley said.

"Then let's take this plane off autopilot," Mary-Kate cheered. "We're headed for Rome!"

CHAPTER TWO
Going Global

"*Ciao, Italia!*" Ashley called from her pilot's seat. She glanced down at her computer printout of fun facts about Italy. "Did you know that Italy produces over 2.75 million tons of pasta each year?"

"I can't wait for lunch!" Mary-Kate said. She opened her special-agent bracelet "Digital diary—Saturday, ten A.M. We are about to land in Rome. First stop, the Global Games!"

Once their plane touched down, Mary-Kate and Ashley hopped on their scooters. When they reached the gymnastics arena, they found a huge crowd outside. Reporters were mobbing the athletes.

"Look!" Mary-Kate said. "There's Romy Bates!" She pointed to a young woman standing behind a microphone. Romy was wearing tight black pants and a short blue and white jacket.

Romy was a brilliant computer whiz— and an international criminal! Mary-Kate and Ashley had run into her on their other assignments.

"What's she doing here?" Ashley asked.

"It looks like she's holding some kind

of a press conference," Mary-Kate said.

"Come on," Ashley said. "We'd better find out what she's up to."

The girls dashed into the press conference.

"My team will take *all* the gold medals," Romy announced to the reporters.

"Romy, why are *you* taking all the credit for the Hipslovian team's performance?" a reporter asked.

"I deserve it," Romy said. "I'm coaching them now."

"*She's* a gymnastics coach?" Ashley whispered. "Since when?"

"Romy, is it true that you are one of the most intelligent people in the world?" a reporter asked.

"Yes," Romy said. "But don't think of me as just a brilliant genius. Think of me as *fun*. I'm lots of ahh-ahhh-ahhh . . ."

"Take cover!" Mary Kate yelled. "Romy's going to sneeze!" She and Ashley ducked behind a stone statue.

"Ah-CHOO!" Romy's sneeze was so tremendous, it blew the wig off one of the reporters standing in front!

"Now, that sneeze was super-powered." Ashley giggled.

"Romy can't help it," Mary-Kate said. "She's allergic to *everything*."

Romy squinted into the crowd. She spotted Mary-Kate and Ashley. "You two!" she snapped. "*You're* not reporters! I'm not answering any of your questions, Special Agent Amber. Or you, Special Agent Misty!"

Romy knew Mary-Kate and Ashley only by their code names.

Romy turned quickly and walked away. The reporters followed close behind.

"That's what *she* thinks," Mary-Kate said. "Whatever she's up to, we're going to shut her down."

"Right," Ashley agreed.

"I have only two questions," Mary-Kate added. "*What* is she up to? And *how* are we going to shut her down?"

Ashley shrugged. "Beats me!"

CHAPTER THREE

A New Routine

"Digital diary—Saturday, twelve P.M. Locker room inside the Global Games. Our disguises are in place. Time to join the fun!" Mary Kate said into her special-agent bracelet.

Ashley adjusted her Team USA leotard. "These clip-cams should help us guard Lauren Andersen—and watch out for Romy Bates." She slipped the tiny camera into her hair.

Mary-Kate did the same thing. She glanced at her reflection in a nearby mirror.

Beside them, Quincy laughed. "It never hurts to look good when you're fighting an evil computer-genius like Romy," he said.

Ashley chuckled. "Now, remember, Quincy, keep a low profile. You're not supposed to talk in front of anyone but us! And besides, gymnastics competitions don't normally allow dogs inside." She lifted him into her backpack.

"Hey! Careful who you're calling a dog, missy." Quincy ducked down inside the pack.

The girls ran out of the locker room

joined the American team at their place
near the balance beam.

A gymnast with short brown hair
jumped up to greet them. "Hi!" the
gymnast whispered. "I'm Lauren
Andersen! You two must be the special
agents. I heard you were going to be here.
Thanks for helping out."

"No problem," Mary-Kate said. "I'm Special Agent Misty. And this is my sister . . ."

"Special Agent Amber," Ashley said.

"We hear you are the best of the best," Mary-Kate said.

Lauren blushed. "I hear you guys are the best, too."

Another girl stepped right in front of Lauren. A girl with a grumpy expression— and big feet.

Grudmilla! Mary-Kate thought. *The Hipslovian team captain!*

"Lauren Andersen is good. But I am better," Grudmilla said. "I will beat her!"

"Hi," Ashley said. "We're the alternates on Lauren's team."

"Nice to meet you," Mary-Kate said. She held out her hand to shake. But Grudmilla ignored her.

"Make a note in your digital diary," Ashley whispered. "Hipslovians are great at gymnastics—but not so good at manners."

"I heard that!" Grudmilla shouted. She glared at Ashley and Mary-Kate. "You two have come late to the games. You didn't go through the warm-ups. Why? Maybe you have something to hide!"

"Uh, no, we don't," Mary-Kate said.

"Yes!" Grudmilla argued. "You do not have a gymnastics routine, do you? If you do, I demand to see it! Or I will go to the officials and ask questions about you!"

Uh-oh! That definitely would not be good! Mary-Kate realized. She and Ashley were only *pretending* to be gymnasts!

"What do we do now?" Ashley whispered to Mary-Kate.

"Well, we *did* take gymnastics," Mary-Kate said.

"Sure—in middle school!" Ashley said. "We're going to tank out there on the mat!"

"No, we're not," Mary-Kate said. "Because I'm not going to let you tank. And you're not going to let me."

"I am waiting!" Grudmilla said. "Let me see your routine—now!"

The twins leaped onto the floor mat. They bowed to each other.

"What do we do now?" Ashley whispered.

Mary-Kate performed a couple of hip-hop moves. Then she pointed at Ashley.

Ashley did a ballet step, then tossed in a spin.

"Good one!" Mary-Kate whispered. "Okay, now—handspring!"

At once, the girls each performed a handspring.

"Keep going! Walk on your hands!" Mary-Kate called.

People in the audience clapped and cheered.

"Okay, time for the big ending!" Ashley said, performing a back flip.

"Catch me!" Mary-Kate whispered. She did a forward flip and landed in Ashley's arms. "Ta-da!" she cried.

The audience exploded with applause. Lauren cheered. Grudmilla folded her arms and frowned.

Mary-Kate bowed to the audience. "Hey! Over there. Look who just came in!" She pointed across the room—at Romy Bates.

"What's going on?" Ashley muttered.
Suddenly, colored smoke filled the air.
"I can't see a thing!" Ashley cried.
"Me, either!" Mary-Kate coughed.

But when the smoke cleared, they could see one thing for sure.

Lauren and Grudmilla were both gone!

CHAPTER FOUR
Missing Gymnasts

"What happened?" Mary-Kate asked.

Ashley saw a piece of paper on the floor. She picked it up.

"Lauren and Grudmilla have been kidnapped!" Ashley gasped.

"No way," Mary-Kate said. "I'll bet Romy is involved in this. We've got to find her!"

"Right," Ashley agreed. "But first we'd better talk to Grudmilla's team." She took a step toward the Hipslovians' bench.

But the gymnasts marched toward the locker rooms. Their faces were cold and still.

"How weird," Ashley said. "Their captain just vanished in a puff of smoke. And they don't look upset at all. It's like they're all robots or something."

"That's it!" Mary-Kate said. "Ashley, you are a genius!"

"Huh? What are you talking about?" Ashley asked.

"Maybe the Hipslovian team has no feelings—because they really *are* robots!" Mary-Kate said. "That would explain all that super-human stuff they can do!"

Ashley's face lit up. "You're right! And that would explain why Romy is their coach! She's a computer programmer. She could program all their routines into their memories."

Mary-Kate thought for a moment. "So if Romy kidnapped Lauren, Romy's team would be guaranteed to win!"

"You're right! But how can we prove that she did it?" Ashley wondered.

"Let's start by checking out the video our cameras picked up," Mary-Kate said.

She plugged the clip-cams into her special-agent bracelet. The video played on the bracelet's small screen.

Mary-Kate hit the "slow" button. She watched Romy press a red button on a large machine. A second later colored smoke billowed into the arena. Romy grabbed Lauren's arm. Then everything went black.

When the smoke cleared, Lauren and Grudmilla had disappeared.

"So that's it!" Mary-Kate said. "Romy and Grudmilla are working together!"

"Let's find them. They can't be far away," Ashley said. Mary-Kate picked up the note Ashley had found again and stared at it.

"Hey, look. There's a stain on this. "Maybe it's a clue."

"Looks like a job for a special-agent's best friend!" Ashley said. She and Mary-Kate ran over to their backpacks.

"Quincy!" Mary-Kate said. "We need your help!"

Quincy stuck his head out of the top of the pack. "What is it this time?" he asked.

"Take a good whiff," Ashley told him. She held the note up to Quincy's nose.

Quincy sniffed the paper and wagged his tail. "Smells like fresh hot cocoa to me," he said.

He took another big whiff. "This cocoa was made with a rare kind of chocolate sprinkles. Find the café that uses these sprinkles. The person you're looking for should be nearby."

"Quincy, you rule!" Ashley cheered.

"Thanks," he said. "Now follow me!"

CHAPTER FIVE
Follow That Cocoa

"It's official," Mary-Kate said. "My hot cocoa limit is twenty-seven cups."

Ashley frowned at the cup of cocoa in her hand. "How many have we had so far?"

"Twenty-eight." Mary-Kate groaned.

At each café the girls visited, they drank a cup of cocoa. Then Quincy sniffed the empty cup. So far, none of the cafés used the rare chocolate sprinkles Quincy had sniffed out.

Mary-Kate poured her twenty-ninth cup of cocoa into a trash can. Quincy stuck his nose into the empty cup.

He nodded his furry head. "That's it!" he said. "That's the same thing I smelled on the note!"

"Romy's headquarters must be nearby," Mary-Kate said.

Ashley searched the street. There was a private art museum across the way. The trash can in front of it was filled with empty hot-chocolate cups!

"I have a hunch that Romy's in there," Ashley said.

"You could be right," Mary-Kate agreed. "Let's give it a try."

The girls zoomed across the street. Quincy followed close behind.

Ashley pulled open the museum door. She and Mary-Kate entered. They found themselves in a small, dark room.

Ashley clicked open her special-agent bracelet. She tapped a few buttons. "According to my records, Romy really likes trapdoors. She's used them in three out of four of her hideouts."

"Thanks for the tip," Mary-Kate said. "Here's my plan: Let's stick as close to the walls as we can."

The girls flattened themselves against a side wall.

Whoosh! The wall suddenly whirled around. It swept the girls into a big hole in the floor!

"Help!" Mary-Kate screamed.

"Ahhhh!" Ashley cried. She, Mary-Kate, and Quincy fell into the basement below.

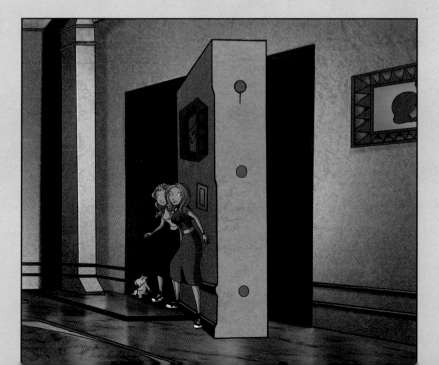

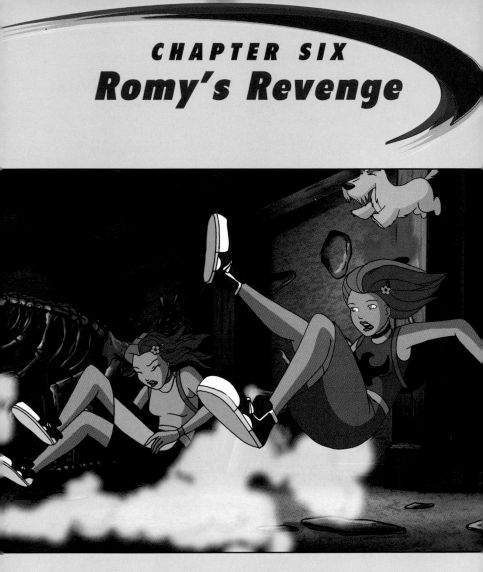

Mary-Kate and Ashley landed with a loud thud. Seconds later Quincy dropped into Ashley's lap.

"Ouch!" Mary-Kate said. She stood up and brushed herself off. She was covered in dust! "Next time *you* make the plan for getting around the trapdoor."

"I will," Ashley agreed. She gulped. "If there *is* a next time!" She glanced around the room. It was filled with spooky cobwebs.

"How do we get out of here?" Quincy asked.

"Well—" Mary-Kate started to answer.

"I *told* you that you wouldn't stop me!" a voice interrupted.

Mary-Kate turned and saw Romy Bates. She was sitting on a throne at the end of the room.

"Why are you doing this?" Mary-Kate asked. "Why are you ruining the Global Games?"

"Because of my allergies I never got to play sports," Romy explained. "All I've

ever wanted was to be a winner. If I can't
win by playing fair, I'll do it by cheating!"

Ashley gasped. "Mary-Kate, look!" She
pointed to a corner of the room. Lauren
was lying on the floor. Grudmilla sat on
top of her, holding her down.

"Will you get off me?" Lauren cried.

"No," Grudmilla answered. "Romy says

you are to be staying put. This is a good way to keep you staying put."

"Lauren is the only person who can keep my team from winning," Romy explained. "So she stays here until the games are over."

"You'll never get away with this," Ashley said.

"Oh, yes, I will." Romy sneered.

Whoosh! The trapdoor above Ashley

and Mary-Kate opened again. The Hipslovian gymnasts dropped down into the room. *Thud! Thud! Thud!*

"My girls will take care of you two special agents," Romy said. "Then they will go back to the games to win the gold medal—for *me*!"

All seven gymnasts put their hands up in a karate pose.

"Watch out!" Mary-Kate called. "They're ready to fight!"

Romy pushed a button on the wall.
Loud marching music began to play. The
Hipslovian gymnasts moved in time to
the music.

Romy turned a dial on the wall. The
music changed. Now it was faster.
Trumpets blared and a loud, steady

drumbeat sounded. The robots charged toward them.

"Ashley!" Mary-Kate cried. "Look out!"

The robots dove at Mary-Kate and Ashley.

KA-POW! Ashley swung her leg up in a karate kick.

CLANG! Two robots fell to the floor.

"Girls, look out!" Quincy yelled.

Mary-Kate and Ashley whirled around.
Five more robots lunged toward them.

"Use a tuck and roll!" Ashley called.
"Go toward those steps!" She pointed
across the dark room to some old brick

steps leading out of the basement.

Mary-Kate and Ashley tucked their bodies into a ball. They rolled toward the steps.

Crash! They knocked the gymnasts over like bowling pins. But five more robots took their places!

All the while the marching music played on.

"This song is driving me crazy!" Ashley yelled. "You'd think Romy would go for something with a hipper beat!"

"The beat! That's it!" Mary-Kate cried. She flipped open her special-agent bracelet and attached the mini clip-cams.

"Oh, please, let there be a salsa station around here!" she said. She turned a dial on her bracelet.

"We're about to be stomped by robots!" Ashley cried. "And you want to listen to *the radio?*"

"Yes!" Mary-Kate cheered. "I found it!" She turned the volume knob way up. The air was filled with loud salsa music.

"Cross your fingers, Ashley. If this doesn't work, we're doomed!"

CHAPTER SEVEN
We've Got the Beat

The salsa song drowned out Romy's marching music. Instantly, the robots looked confused. They began walking in circles and banging into walls.

"Hey! It's working!" Ashley cheered.

The robots shuddered. Black smoke drifted up from their heads.

KA-BLAM! The robots exploded.

"Awesome!" Mary-Kate cried.

"Stop them!" Grudmilla ordered. "They are escaping!"

"I am a very evil person," Romy said. "And you two special agents are really starting to get on my nerves."

"Yes!" Grudmilla said. "Time to be using your secret weapon to finish them off!"

Ashley glanced down at her clothes. She and Mary-Kate were still covered with dust. "Hey," she said to her sister. "I'm thinking of a word . . ."

"Is that word 'allergies'?" Mary-Kate asked.

Ashley nodded. Both girls ran toward each other. They bumped their bellies together. A cloud of white dust flew up into the air.

"Ahhh-chooo!" Romy sneezed.

Her sneeze was so huge, it sent her flying backward. "Ahhhh-choo!" Romy sneezed again and slammed into Grudmilla.

"Whoa!" Grudmilla tumbled off Lauren's back.

Mary-Kate and Ashley bumped bellies again.

This time, Romy sneezed so hard, she sent Grudmilla sailing into a wall.

Grudmilla was knocked out cold.

"You two have ruined . . . ah-choo . . . everything!" Romy cried. "I'll . . . I'll ah-choo. . . get you for this!"

"Come on!" Ashley called to Lauren. "The gymnastics competition is about to start!"

Lauren, Ashley, Mary-Kate, and Quincy raced up the brick steps. They hurried to the sports arena.

"Mary-Kate, how did you do that?" Ashley asked on the way.

"I figured out how Romy was controlling the robots—with music!" Mary-Kate explained. "But all the music Romy used had regular beats. Then I remembered my salsa disk from the plane. I thought maybe salsa music, with its jerky beat, would confuse the robots."

"And it worked!" Ashley said. "Beautifully!"

They reached the arena just in time for the gymnastics events to start.

Lauren hurried to her place. Ashley, Mary-Kate, and Quincy took seats in the audience.

Lauren approached the balance beam and started her routine. She did a perfect double back tuck. The crowd cheered and clapped.

"This is so cool!" Mary-Kate said. "Lauren gets to compete fairly. And Romy and Grudmilla are banned for life from gymnastics."

"And look!" Ashley said. "Lauren just scored a perfect ten on the balance beam!"

The crowd cheered as Lauren received the gold medal. Then she stepped up to the microphone. "I want to thank my new

friends, Misty and Amber. They made it possible for me to be here and win the gold," she announced.

"We were happy to help," Mary-Kate said.

"It was easy," Ashley added, "with my super-powered sister by my side!"

Quincy wagged his tail and hopped into Mary-Kate's arms. "Sometimes, you girls really know how to make a dog proud!" he said.

Let's go save
the world . . . again!

MARY-KATE AND ASHLEY
IN ACTION!

Book #3
Fubble Bubble Trouble

URGENT MESSAGE

FROM: Headquarters

TO: Special Agents Misty and Amber

LOCATION: The Mall of Malls

PROBLEM: A new candy called Fubble d'Bubble is interfering with TV reception all across the country!

YOUR MISSION: Go undercover as candy-makers at the Fubble d'Bubble factory in The Mall of Malls to find out who or what is causing all the static!

mary-kateandashley

a whole new book

MARY-KATE AND ASHLEY
in ACTION!

look for other books in this
brand-new book series

LOOK FOR
MARY-KATE AND ASHLEY in ACTION! #3
FUBBLE BUBBLE TROUBLE
COMING SOON!

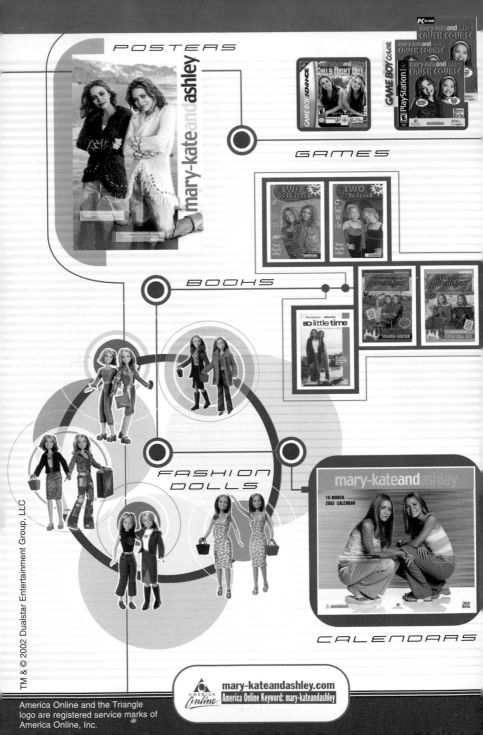

POSTERS

GAMES

BOOKS

FASHION DOLLS

CALENDARS

mary-kateandashley.com
America Online Keyword: mary-kateandashley

ENTER BELOW FOR YOUR CHANCE TO WIN A FRAMED, AUTOGRAPHED

MARY-KATE AND ASHLEY in ACTION!

ANIMATED IMAGE!*

*Prize may differ from image shown above

Mail to: **MARY-KATE AND ASHLEY in ACTION!**
WIN COOL MARY-KATE AND ASHLEY
in ACTION! PRIZES SWEEPSTAKES
C/O HarperEntertainment
Attention: Children's Marketing Department
10 East 53rd Street, New York, NY 10022

No purchase necessary.

Name: _____

Address: _____

City: _____ State: _____ Zip: _____

Phone: _____ Age: _____

HarperEntertainment
An Imprint of HarperCollinsPublishers
www.harpercollins.com

Total Books for Real Girls.

PARACHUTE PRESS

D
DUALSTAR
PUBLICATIONS